Simple Machines to the Rescue

Wedges to the Rescue

by Sharon Thales

Consultant:
Louis A. Bloomfield, PhD
Professor of Physics
University of Virginia
Charlottesville, Virginia

Mankato, Minnesota

First Facts is published by Capstone Press,
151 Good Counsel Drive, P.O. Box 669, Mankato, Minnesota 56002.
www.capstonepress.com

Printed in the United States of America

Library of Congress Cataloging-in-Publication Data
Thales, Sharon.
Wedges to the rescue / Sharon Thales.
p. cm.—(First facts. Simple machines to the rescue)
Summary: "Describes wedges, including what they are, how they work, past uses, and common uses of these simple machines today"—Provided by publisher.
Includes bibliographical references and index.
ISBN-13: 978-0-7368-6750-4 (hardcover)
ISBN-10: 0-7368-6750-3 (hardcover)
1. Wedges—Juvenile literature. I. Title. II. Series.
TJ1201.W44T43 2007
621.8—dc22 2006021495

Editorial Credits
Becky Viaene, editor; Thomas Emery, designer; Jo Miller, photo researcher/photo editor

Photo Credits
Capstone Press/Karon Dubke, cover, 5, 12 (both), 13, 17, 18–19, 21 (all)
Corbis/Cory Sorensen, 14–15; zefa/Norman, 20
Corel, 8–9
Getty Images Inc./Iconica/Peter Dawson, 6
North Wind Picture Archives, 11

1 2 3 4 5 6 12 11 10 09 08 07

Table of Contents

A Helpful Wedge

It's snack time, but there's a problem. Two hungry people want to share one apple. How can they split it into two equal pieces?

Wedge to the rescue!

A knife is a helpful **wedge**. Its sharp blade quickly cuts the apple into pieces to share.

Work It

A wedge is a **simple machine**. Simple machines have one or no moving parts. Machines are used to make **work** easier.

Work is using a **force** to move an object. Wedges do work by splitting things apart. They are also used to push things together. Since ancient times, people have used wedges to make work easier.

Wedge Fact

A wedge is wide at one end. It slopes to a narrow point at the other end. But shape alone does not make something a wedge. A wedge must do work.

A Wedge in Time

Ancient Egyptians needed a way to split huge blocks of stone to make pyramids. They hammered wooden wedges into cracks in the stone and poured water onto the wedges. The water soaked into the wedges and made them bigger. The wedges pushed the cracks open wider until the blocks split into pieces.

People have used wedges since ancient times to clean animal skins. First, they used sharp rock wedges to scrape meat from the skin. Years later, they used metal knives or scrapers. Today, people still use wedges to clean animal skins.

What Would We Do Without Wedges?

Wedges make it easier to do today's work too. Zippers have wedges that help you open and close a backpack. The slide's wedges push the wedged teeth together or split them apart.

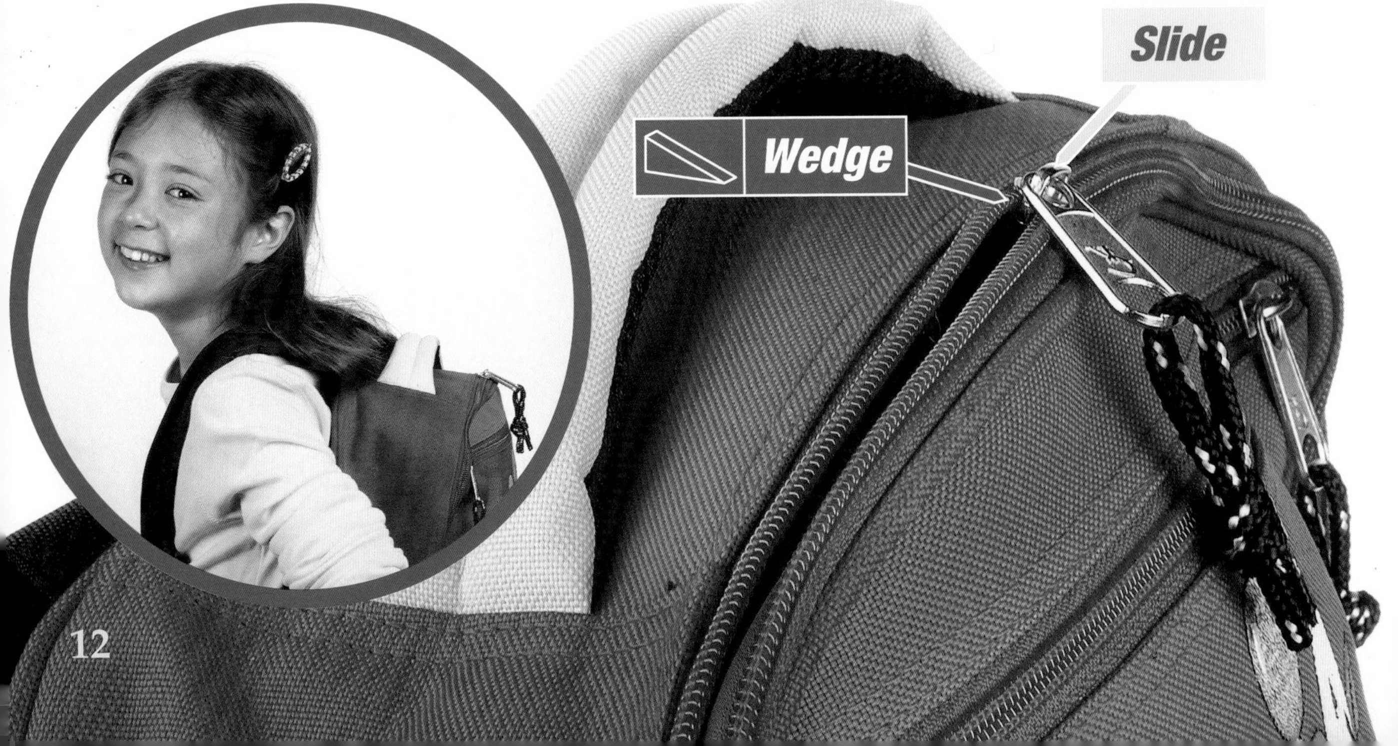

Slide

Wedge

Wedges also help keep doors open. A doorstop pushes up on the bottom of a door. This wedge holds the door and floor together so the door won't move.

Axes are also wedges. They help split large pieces of wood into small pieces. Whenever people need to cut something, they can grab a wedge.

Wedge Fact

Firefighters use axes to cut through doors and roofs. These wedges help firefighters save people from burning buildings.

Working Together

A can opener is a **complex machine.** It is made of several simple machines. To use a can opener, you squeeze two levers together. This action pushes the wedge into the can. When you turn the handle, wheels and axles turn the wedge to cut the can.

Wedge Buddies

Six kinds of simple machines combine to make almost every machine there is.

- **Inclined plane**–a slanting surface that is used to move objects to different levels
- **Lever**–a bar that turns on a resting point and is used to lift items
- **Pulley**–a grooved wheel turned by a rope, belt, or chain that often moves heavy objects
- **Screw**–an inclined plane wrapped around a post that usually holds objects together
- **Wedge**–an inclined plane that moves to split things apart or push them together
- **Wheel and axle**–a wheel that turns around a bar to move objects

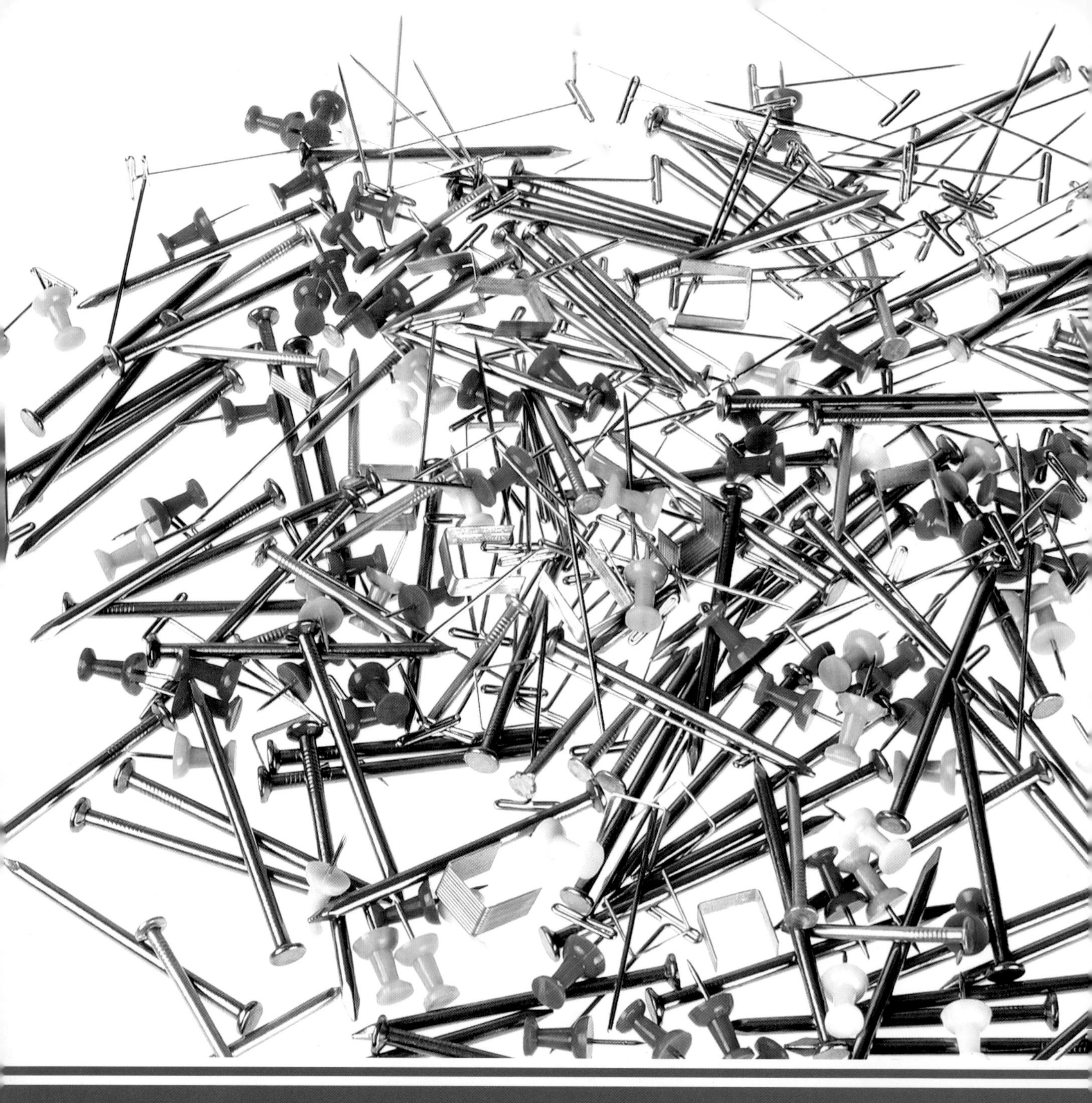

Wedges Everywhere

Whether you're at home, at school, inside, or outside, wedges are never far away. Nails are wedges. Needles, staples, and push pins are wedges too. You never know when one of these tiny wedges will save the day.

Amazing but True!

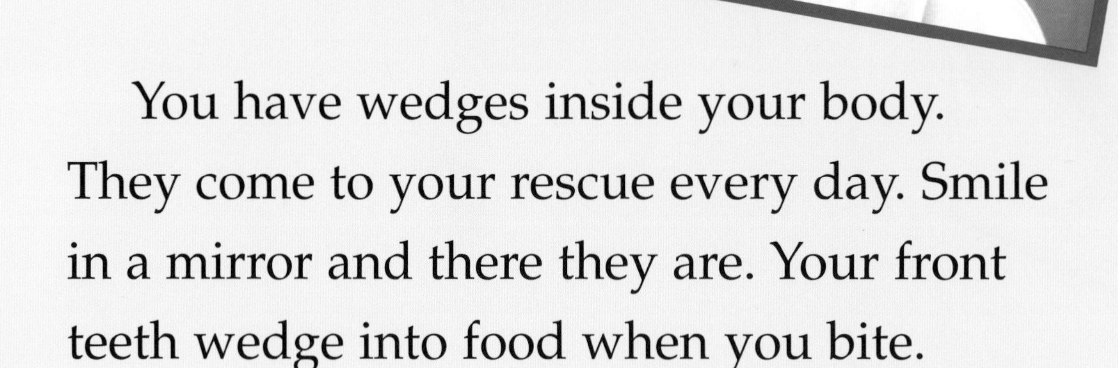

You have wedges inside your body. They come to your rescue every day. Smile in a mirror and there they are. Your front teeth wedge into food when you bite.

Hands On: Working with a Wedge

What You Need

4-by-8-inch (10-by-20-centimeter) piece of cardboard, pencil, ruler, scissors, telephone book

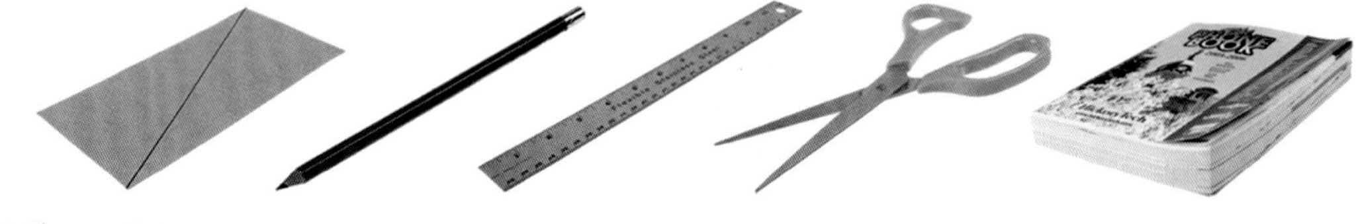

What You Do

1. Measure the cardboard and draw a diagonal line on it from one corner to another corner.
2. Cut along the line. You now have two cardboard wedges.
3. Pick up one of the cardboard wedges. Open the phone book just enough to rest the tip of the long point of the wedge inside.
4. Push the wedge toward the inside of the phone book.

You used the wedge to do work. You applied force by pushing the wide edge of the wedge. The force opened the phone book by moving the pages apart.

Glossary

complex machine (KOM-pleks muh-SHEEN)—a machine made of two or more simple machines

force (FORSS)—a push or a pull

simple machine (SIM-puhl muh-SHEEN)—a tool with one or no moving parts that moves an object when you push or pull; wedges are simple machines.

wedge (WEDGE)—an inclined plane that moves to split things apart or push them together

work (WURK)—when a force moves an object

Read More

Dahl, Michael. *Cut, Chop, and Stop: A Book about Wedges.* Amazing Science. Minneapolis: Picture Window Books, 2006.

Oxlade, Chris. *Ramps and Wedges.* Useful Machines. Chicago: Heinemann Library, 2003.

Tieck, Sarah. *Wedges.* Simple Machines. Edina, Minn.: Abdo, 2006.

Internet Sites

FactHound offers a safe, fun way to find Internet sites related to this book. All of the sites on FactHound have been researched by our staff.

Here's how:

1. Visit *www.facthound.com*
2. Choose your grade level.
3. Type in this book ID **0736867503** for age-appropriate sites. You may also browse subjects by clicking on letters, or by clicking on pictures and words.

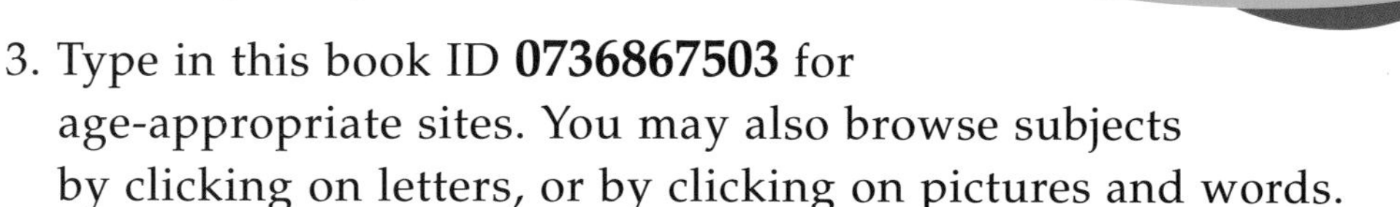

4. Click on the **Fetch It** button.

FactHound will fetch the best sites for you!

Index